MAY 05

"Marshes must be something like swamps," ventured
Peter Rabbit. Frontispiece. *See page 13.*

The Adventures of Poor Mrs. Quack

THORNTON W. BURGESS

Original Illustrations by Harrison Cady
Adapted by Thea Kliros

PUBLISHED IN ASSOCIATION WITH THE
THORNTON W. BURGESS MUSEUM AND THE
GREEN BRIAR NATURE CENTER, SANDWICH, MASSACHUSETTS,
BY
DOVER PUBLICATIONS, INC., NEW YORK

DOVER CHILDREN'S THRIFT CLASSICS

EDITOR: PHILIP SMITH

Copyright

Published in Canada by General Publishing Company, Ltd., 30 Lesmill Road, Don Mills, Toronto, Ontario.

Published in the United Kingdom by Constable and Company, Ltd., 3 The Lanchesters, 162–164 Fulham Palace Road, London W6 9ER.

Bibliographical Note

This Dover edition, first published in 1993 in association with the Thornton W. Burgess Museum and the Green Briar Nature Center, Sandwich, Massachusetts, who have provided a new introduction, is an unabridged republication of the work first published by Little, Brown, and Company, Boston, in 1917. The original halftone illustrations by Harrison Cady have been adapted in line format by Thea Kliros for this edition.

Library of Congress Cataloging-in-Publication Data

Burgess, Thornton W. (Thornton Waldo), 1874–1965.
   The adventures of poor Mrs. Quack / Thornton W. Burgess ; original illustrations by Harrison Cady adapted by Thea Kliros.
      p.   cm. — (Dover children's thrift classics)
   Summary: Separated from her husband and driven from her home by hunters, Mrs. Quack finds refuge with the animals of the Green Forest.
   ISBN 0-486-27818-2 (pbk.)
   [1. Ducks—Fiction. 2. Animals—Fiction. 3. Hunting—Fiction.]
I. Cady, Harrison, 1877–   ill. II. Kliros, Thea, ill. III. Title.
IV. Series.
PZ7.B917Af 1993
[Fic]—dc20   93-25382
                                           CIP
                                         AC

Manufactured in the United States of America
Dover Publications, Inc., 31 East 2nd Street, Mineola, N.Y. 11501

Introduction to the Dover Edition

The Adventures of Poor Mrs. Quack was written by Thornton W. Burgess in 1916 at a time when the wild duck population of the United States faced serious threat of extermination. There were no laws establishing seasons, limits or methods for duck hunting. The result was that some species were nearly gone. The campaign to end this situation was long and bitter. Even some naturalists of the day were opposed to it. Yet Thornton Burgess decided to do what he could, even though he was assailed for his part. Thus was born this book about Mrs. Quack the Mallard Duck.

Mrs. Quack, along with Mr. Quack and their neighbors, is forced by hunters to leave her home on the Big River and seek a safer retreat. She finally arrives, alone, at the Smiling Pool, where she is befriended by Peter Rabbit and the animals of the dear Old Briarpatch (called "Quaddies," or quadrupeds). She tells them of the horrible guns of the hunters, the death of many of her friends and the disappearance of Mr. Quack along the way. She believes Mr. Quack is still alive, and the creatures of the forest and pond decide to help her. With the aid of Sammy Jay and Blacky the Crow, they are able to rescue Mr. Quack and reunite the pair, and so the Quacks—and eventually ten little Quacks—become residents of the Green Forest.

This story and others by Thornton Burgess, along with books, papers, photographs and memorabilia of his life, are part of the collections of the Thornton W. Burgess Society in Sandwich, Massachusetts, on Cape Cod, and are displayed at the Burgess Museum there. This is the town where Burgess spent his youth and discovered the Smiling Pool and dear Old Briar-patch of his stories. The Society, which was formed in 1976, also maintains a widely used environmental education center in order to carry out the goals that Burgess espoused throughout his life.

Contents

List of Illustrations

I

Peter Rabbit Becomes Acquainted with Mrs. Quack

Make a new acquaintance every time
  you can;
You'll find it interesting and a very help-
  ful plan.

IT MEANS MORE knowledge. You cannot meet any one without learning something from him if you keep your ears open and your eyes open. Every one is at least a little different from every one else, and the more people you know, the more you may learn. Peter Rabbit knows this, and that is one reason he always is so eager to find out about other people. He had left Jimmy Skunk and Bobby Coon in the Green Forest and had headed for the Smiling Pool to see if Grandfather Frog was awake yet. He had no idea of meeting a stranger there, and so you can imagine just how surprised he was when he got in sight of the Smiling Pool to see some one whom he never had seen before swimming about there. He knew right away who it was. He knew that it was Mrs. Quack the Duck, because he had often heard about her. And then, too, it was very clear from her looks that she was a cousin of the ducks he had seen in Farmer Brown's dooryard. The difference was that while they were big and white and stupid-looking, Mrs. Quack was smaller, brown, very trim, and looked anything but stupid.

Peter was so surprised to see her in the Smiling Pool that he almost forgot to be polite. I am afraid he stared in a very impolite way as he hurried to the edge of the bank. "I suppose," said Peter, "that you are Mrs. Quack, but I never expected to see you unless I should go over to the Big River, and that is a place I never have visited and hardly expect to because it is too far from the dear Old Briar-patch. You are Mrs. Quack, aren't you?"

"Yes," replied Mrs. Quack, "and you must be Peter Rabbit. I've heard of you very often." All the time Mrs. Quack was swimming back and forth and in little circles in the most uneasy way.

"I hope you've heard nothing but good of me," replied Peter.

Mrs. Quack stopped her uneasy swimming

for a minute and almost smiled as she looked at Peter. "The worst I have heard is that you are very curious about other people's affairs," said she.

Peter looked a wee, wee bit foolish, and then he laughed right out. "I guess that is true enough," said he. "I like to learn all I can, and how can I learn without being curious? I'm curious right now. I'm wondering what brings you to the Smiling Pool when you never have been here before. It is the last place in the world I ever expected to find you."

"That's why I'm here," replied Mrs. Quack. "I hope others feel the same way. I came here because I just *had* to find some place where people wouldn't expect to find me and so wouldn't come looking for me. Little Joe Otter saw me yesterday on the Big River and told me of this place, and so, because I just had to go somewhere, I came here."

Peter's eyes opened very wide with surprise. "Why," he exclaimed, "I should think you would be perfectly safe on the Big River! I don't see how any harm can possibly come to you out there."

The words were no sooner out of Peter's mouth than a faint bang sounded from way off towards the Big River. Mrs. Quack gave a great start and half lifted her wings as if to fly.

But she thought better of it, and then Peter saw that she was trembling all over.

"Did you hear that?" she asked in a faint voice.

Peter nodded. "That was a gun, a terrible gun, but it was a long way from here," said he.

"It was over on the Big River," said Mrs. Quack. "That's why it isn't safe for me over there. That's why I just had to find some other place. Oh, dear, the very sound of a gun sets me to shaking and makes my heart feel as if it would stop beating. Are you sure I am perfectly safe here?"

"Perfectly," spoke up Jerry Muskrat, who had been listening from the top of the Big Rock, where he was lunching on a clam, "unless you are not smart enough to keep out of the clutches of Reddy Fox or Old Man Coyote or Hooty the Owl or Redtail the Hawk."

"I'm not afraid of *them*," declared Mrs. Quack. "It's those two-legged creatures with terrible guns I'm afraid of," and she began to swim about more uneasily than ever.

II
Mrs. Quack Is Distrustful

JERRY MUSKRAT THINKS there is no place in the world like the Smiling Pool. So, for the matter of that, does Grandfather Frog and also Spotty the Turtle. You see, they have spent their lives there and know little about the rest of the Great World. When Mrs. Quack explained that all she feared was that a two-legged creature with a terrible gun might find her there, Jerry Muskrat hastened to tell her that she had nothing to worry about on that account.

"No one hunts here now that Farmer Brown's boy has put away his terrible gun," explained Jerry. "There was a time when he used to hunt here and set traps, which are worse than terrible guns, but that was long ago, before he knew any better."

"Who is Farmer Brown's boy?" demanded Mrs. Quack, looking more anxious than ever. "Is he one of those two-legged creatures?"

"Yes," said Peter Rabbit, who had been listening with all his ears, "but he is the best friend we Quaddies have got. He is such a good friend that he ought to be a Quaddy himself. Why, this last winter he fed some of us when food was scarce, and he saved Mrs. Grouse when she was caught in a snare, which you know is a kind of trap. He won't let any harm come to you here, Mrs. Quack."

"I wouldn't trust him, not for one single little minute," declared Mrs. Quack. "I wouldn't trust one of those two-legged creatures, not *one*. You say he fed some of you last winter, but that doesn't mean anything good. Do you know what I've known these two-legged creatures to do?"

"What?" demanded Peter and Jerry together.

"I've known them to scatter food where we Ducks would be sure to find it and to take the greatest care that nothing should frighten us while we were eating. And then, after we had got in the habit of feeding in that particular place and had grown to feel perfectly safe there, they have hidden close by until a lot of us were feeding together and then fired their terrible guns and killed a lot of my friends and dreadfully hurt a lot more. I wouldn't trust one of them, not *one!*"

"Oh, how dreadful!" cried Peter, looking

quite as shocked as he felt. Then he added eagerly, "But our Farmer Brown's boy wouldn't do anything like that. You haven't the least thing to fear from him."

"Perhaps not," said Mrs. Quack, shaking her head doubtfully, "but I wouldn't trust him. I wouldn't trust him as far off as I could see him. The Smiling Pool is a very nice place, although it is dreadfully small, but if Farmer Brown's boy is likely to come over here, I guess I better look for some other place, though goodness knows where I will find one where I will feel perfectly safe."

"You are safe right here, if you have sense enough to stay here," declared Jerry Muskrat rather testily. "Don't you suppose Peter and I know what we are talking about?"

"I wish I could believe so," returned Mrs. Quack sadly, "but if you had been through what I've been through, and suffered what I've suffered, you wouldn't believe any place safe, and you certainly wouldn't trust one of those two-legged creatures. Why, for weeks they haven't given me a chance to get a square meal, and—and—I don't know what has become of Mr. Quack, and I'm all alone!" There was a little sob in her voice and tears in her eyes.

"Tell us all about it," begged Peter. "Perhaps we can help you."

III

Mrs. Quack Tells About Her Home

"IT'S A LONG story," said Mrs. Quack, shaking the tears from her eyes, "and I hardly know where to begin."

"Begin at the beginning," said Jerry Muskrat. "Your home is somewhere way up in the Northland where Honker the Goose lives, isn't it?"

Mrs. Quack nodded. "I wish I were there this very minute," she replied, the tears coming again. "But sometimes I doubt if ever I'll get there again. You folks who don't have to leave your homes every year don't know how well off you are or how much you have to be thankful for."

"I never could understand what people want to leave their homes for, anyway," declared Peter.

"We don't leave because we want to, but because we *have* to," replied Mrs. Quack, "and

8

we go back just as soon as we can. What would you do if you couldn't find a single thing to eat?"

"I guess I'd starve," replied Peter simply.

"I guess you would, and that is just what we would do, if we didn't take the long journey south when Jack Frost freezes everything tight up there where my home is," returned Mrs. Quack. "He comes earlier up there and stays twice as long as he does here, and makes ten times as much ice and snow. We get most of our food in the water or in the mud under the water, as of course you know, and when the water is frozen, there isn't a scrap of anything we can get to eat. We just *have* to come south. It isn't because we want to, but because we must! There is nothing else for us to do."

"Then I don't see what you want to make your home in such a place for," said practical Peter. "I should think you would make it where you can live all the year around."

"I was born up there, and I love it just as you love the dear Old Briar-patch," replied Mrs. Quack simply. "It is home, and there is no place like home. Besides, it is a very beautiful and a very wonderful place in summer. There is everything that Ducks and Geese love. We have all we want of the food we love best. Everywhere is shallow water with tall grass growing in it."

"Huh!" interrupted Peter, "I wouldn't think much of a place like that."

"That's because you don't know what is good," snapped Jerry Muskrat. "It would suit me," he added, with shining eyes.

"There are the dearest little islands just made for safe nesting-places," continued Mrs. Quack, without heeding the interruptions. "And the days are long, and it is easy to hide, and there is nothing to fear, for two-legged creatures with terrible guns never come there."

"If there is nothing to fear, why do you care about places to hide?" demanded Peter.

"Well, of course, we have enemies, just as you do here, but they are natural enemies,— Foxes and Minks and Hawks and Owls," explained Mrs. Quack. "Of course, we have to watch out for them and have places where we can hide from them, but it is our wits against their wits, and it is our own fault if we get caught. That is perfectly fair, so we don't mind that. It is only men who are not fair. They don't know what fairness is."

Peter nodded that he understood, and Mrs. Quack went on. "Last summer Mr. Quack and

I had our nest on the dearest little island, and no one found it. First we had twelve eggs, and then twelve of the dearest babies you ever saw."

"Maybe," said Peter doubtfully, thinking of his own babies.

"They grew so fast that by the time the cold weather came, they were as big as their father and mother," continued Mrs. Quack. "And they were smart, too. They had learned how to take care of themselves just as well as I could. I certainly was proud of that family. But now I don't know where one of them is."

Mrs. Quack suddenly choked up with grief, and Peter Rabbit politely turned his head away.

IV

Mrs. Quack Continues Her Story

WHEN MRS. QUACK told of her twelve children and how she didn't know where one of them was, Peter Rabbit and Jerry Muskrat knew just how badly she was feeling, and they turned their heads away and pretended that they didn't see her tears. In a few minutes she bravely went on with her story.

"When Jack Frost came and we knew it was time to begin the long journey, Mr. Quack and myself and our twelve children joined with some other Duck families, and with Mr. Quack in the lead, we started for our winter home, which really isn't a home but just a place to stay. For a while we had nothing much to fear. We would fly by day and at night rest in some quiet lake or pond or on some river, with the Great Woods all about us or sometimes great marshes. Perhaps you don't know what marshes are. If the Green Meadows here had little streams of water running every which way through them, and the ground was all soft and muddy and full of water, and the grass grew tall, they would be marshes."

Jerry Muskrat's eyes sparkled. "I would like a place like that!" he exclaimed.

"You certainly would," replied Mrs. Quack. "We always find lots of your relatives in such places."

"Marshes must be something like swamps," ventured Peter Rabbit, who had been thinking the matter over.

"Very much the same, only with grass and rushes in place of trees and bushes," replied Mrs. Quack. "There is plenty to eat and the loveliest hiding-places. In some of these we stayed days at a time. In fact, we stayed until Jack Frost came to drive us out. Then as we flew, we began to see the homes of these terrible two-legged creatures called men, and from that time on we never knew a minute of peace, excepting when we were flying high in the air or far out over the water. If we could have just kept flying all the time or never had to go near the shore, we would have been all right. But we had to eat."

"Of course," said Peter. "Everybody has to eat."

"And we had to rest," said Mrs. Quack.

"Certainly," said Peter. "Everybody has to do that."

"And to eat we had to go in close to shore where the water was not at all deep, because it is only in such places that we can get food," continued Mrs. Quack. "It takes a lot of strength to fly as we fly, and strength requires plenty of food. Mr. Quack knew all the best feeding-places, for he had made the long journey several times, so every day he would lead the way to one of these. He always chose the wildest and most lonely looking places he could find, as far as possible from the homes of men, but even then he was never careless. He would lead us around back and forth over the place he had chosen, and we would all look with all our might for signs of danger. If we saw none, we would drop down a little nearer and a little nearer. But with all our watchfulness, we never could be sure, absolutely sure, that all was safe. Sometimes those terrible two-legged creatures would be hiding in the very middle of the wildest, most lonely looking marshes. They would be covered with grass so that we couldn't see them. Then, as we flew over them, would come the bang, bang, bang, bang of terrible guns, and always some of our flock would drop. We would have to leave them behind, for we knew if we wanted to live we must get beyond the reach of those terrible guns. So we would fly our hardest. It was awful, just simply awful!"

Mrs. Quack paused and shuddered, and Peter Rabbit and Jerry Muskrat shuddered in sympathy.

"Sometimes we would have to try three or four feeding-places before we found one where there were no terrible guns. And when we did find one, we would be so tired and frightened that we couldn't enjoy our food, and we didn't dare to sleep without some one on watch all the time. It was like that every day. The farther we got, the worse it became. Our flock grew smaller and smaller. Those who escaped the terrible guns would be so frightened that they would forget to follow their leader and would fly in different directions and later perhaps join other flocks. So it was that when at last we reached the place in the sunny Southland for which we had started, Mr. Quack and I were alone. What became of our twelve children I don't know. I am afraid the terrible guns killed some. I hope some joined other flocks and escaped, but I don't know."

"I hope they did too," said Peter.

V

Peter Learns More of Mrs. Quack's Troubles

It often happens when we know
　The troubles that our friends pass
　　through,
Our own seem very small indeed;
　You'll always find that this is true.

"MY, YOU MUST have felt glad when you reached your winter home!" exclaimed Peter Rabbit when Mrs. Quack finished the account of her long, terrible journey from her summer home in the far Northland to her winter home in the far Southland.

"I did," replied Mrs. Quack, "but all the time I couldn't forget those to whom terrible things had happened on the way down, and then, too, I kept dreading the long journey back."

"I don't see why you didn't stay right there. I would have," said Peter, nodding his head with an air of great wisdom.

"Not if you were I," replied Mrs. Quack. "In the first place it isn't a proper place in which to bring up young Ducks and make them strong and healthy. In the second place there are more dangers down there for young Ducks than up in the far Northland. In the third place there isn't room for all the Ducks to nest properly. And lastly there is a great longing for our real home, which Old Mother Nature has put in our hearts and which just *makes* us go. We couldn't be happy if we didn't."

"Is the journey back as bad as the journey down?" asked Peter.

"Worse, very much worse," replied Mrs. Quack sadly. "You can see for yourself just how bad it is, for here I am all alone." Tears filled Mrs. Quack's eyes. "It is almost too terrible to talk about," she continued after a minute. "You see, for one thing, food isn't as plentiful as it is in the fall, and we just have to go wherever it is to be found. Those two-legged creatures know where those feeding-grounds are just as well as we do, and they hide there with their terrible guns just as they did when we were coming south. But it is much worse now, very much worse. You see, when we were going the other way, if we found them at one place we could go on to another, but when we are going north we cannot always do that. We cannot go any faster than Jack Frost does. Sometimes we are driven out of a place by the bang, bang of the terrible guns and go on, only to find that we have caught up with Jack Frost, and that the ponds and the rivers are still covered with ice. Then there is nothing to do but to turn back to where those terrible guns are waiting for us. We just *have* to do it."

Mrs. Quack stopped and shivered. "It seems to me I have heard nothing but the noise of those terrible guns ever since we started," said she. "I haven't had a good square meal for days and days, nor a good rest. That is what makes me so dreadfully nervous. Sometimes, when we had been driven from place to place until we had caught up with Jack Frost, there would be nothing but ice excepting in small places in a river where the water runs too swiftly to freeze. We would just have to drop into one of these to rest a little, because we had flown so far that our wings ached as if they would drop off. Then just as we would think we were safe for a little while, there would come the bang of a terrible gun. Then we would have to fly again as long as we could, and finally come back to the same place because there was no other place where we could go. Then we would have to do it all over again until night came. Sometimes I think that those men with terrible guns must hate us and want to kill every one of us. If they didn't, they would have a little bit of pity. They simply haven't any hearts at all."

"It does seem so," agreed Peter. "But wait until you know Farmer Brown's boy! *He's* got a heart!" he added brightly.

"I don't want to know him," retorted Mrs. Quack. "If he comes near here, you'll see me leave in a hurry. I wouldn't trust one of them, not one minute. You don't think he will come, do you?"

Peter sat up and looked across the Green Meadows, and his heart sank. "He's coming now, but I'm sure he won't hurt you, Mrs. Quack," said he.

But Mrs. Quack wouldn't wait to see. With a hasty promise to come back when the way was clear, she jumped into the air and on swift wings disappeared towards the Big River.

VI

Farmer Brown's Boy Visits the
Smiling Pool

FARMER BROWN'S BOY had heard Welcome Robin singing in the Old Orchard quite as soon as Peter Rabbit had, and that song of "Cheer up! Cheer up! Cheer up! Cheer!" had awakened quite as much gladness in his heart as it had in Peter's heart. It meant that Mistress Spring really had arrived, and that over in the Green Forest and down on the Green Meadows there would soon be shy blue, and just as shy white violets to look for, and other flowers almost if not quite as sweet and lovely. It meant that his feathered friends would soon be busy house-hunting and building. It meant that his little friends in fur would also be doing something very similar, if they had not already done so. It meant that soon there would be a million lovely things to see and a million joyous sounds to hear.

So the sound of Welcome Robin's voice

made the heart of Farmer Brown's boy even more happy than it was before, and as Welcome Robin just *had* to sing, so Farmer Brown's boy just *had* to whistle. When his work was finished, it seemed to Farmer Brown's boy that something was calling him, calling him to get out on the Green Meadows or over in the Green Forest and share in the happiness of all the little people there. So presently he decided that he would go down to the Smiling Pool to find out how Jerry Muskrat was, and if Grandfather Frog was awake yet, and if the sweet singers of the Smiling Pool had begun their wonderful spring chorus.

Down the Crooked Little Path across the Green Meadows he tramped, and as he drew near the Smiling Pool, he stopped whistling lest the sound should frighten some of the little people there. He was still some distance from the Smiling Pool when out of it sprang a big bird and on swift, whistling wings flew away in the direction of the Big River. Farmer Brown's boy stopped and watched until the bird had disappeared, and on his face was a look of great surprise.

"As I live, that was a Duck!" he exclaimed. "That is the first time I've ever known a wild Duck to be in the Smiling Pool. I wonder what under the sun could have brought her over here."

Just then there was a distant bang in the direction of the Big River. Farmer Brown's boy scowled, and it made his face very angry-looking. "That's it," he muttered. "Hunters are shooting the Ducks on their way north and have driven the poor things to look for any little mudhole where they can get a little rest. Probably that Duck has been shot at so many times on the Big River that she felt safer over here in the Smiling Pool, little as it is."

Farmer Brown's boy had guessed exactly right, as you and I know, and as Peter Rabbit and Jerry Muskrat knew. "It's a shame, a downright shame that any one should want to shoot birds on their way to their nesting-grounds and that the law should let them if they do want to. Some people haven't any hearts; they're all stomachs. I hope that fellow who shot just now over there on the Big River didn't hit anything, and I wish that gun of his might have kicked a little sense of what is right and fair into his head, but of course it didn't."

He grinned at the idea, and then he continued his way towards the Smiling Pool. He hoped he might find another Duck there, and he approached the Smiling Pool very, very carefully.

But when he reached a point where he could see all over the Smiling Pool, there was no one to be seen save Jerry Muskrat sitting on the Big Rock and Peter Rabbit on the bank on the other side. Farmer Brown's boy smiled when he saw them. "Hello, Jerry Muskrat!" said he. "I wonder how a bite of carrot would taste to you." He felt in his pocket and brought out a couple of carrots. One he put on a little tussock in the water where he knew Jerry would find it. The other he tossed across the Smiling Pool where he felt sure Peter would find it. Presently he noticed two or three feathers on the water close to the edge of the bank. Mrs. Quack had left them there. "I believe that was a Mallard Duck," said he, as he studied them. "I know what I'll do. I'll go straight back home and get some wheat and corn and put it here on the edge of the Smiling Pool. Perhaps she will come back and find it."

And this is just what Farmer Brown's boy did.

VII

Mrs. Quack Returns

PETER RABBIT JUST couldn't go back to the dear Old Briar-patch. He just *had* to know if Mrs. Quack would come back to the Smiling Pool. He had seen Farmer Brown's boy come there a second time and scatter wheat and corn among the brown stalks of last summer's rushes, and he had guessed why Farmer Brown's boy had done this. He had guessed that they had been put there especially for Mrs. Quack, and if she should come back as she had promised to do, he wanted to be on hand when she found those good things to eat and hear what she would say.

So Peter stayed over near the Smiling Pool and hoped with all his might that Reddy Fox or Old Man Coyote would not take it into his head to come hunting over there. As luck would have it, neither of them did, and Peter had a very pleasant time gossiping with Jerry

Several times she circled around, high over the
Smiling Pool. *Page 26.*

Muskrat, listening to the sweet voices of unseen singers in the Smiling Pool,—the Hylas, which some people call peepers,—and eating the carrot which Farmer Brown's boy had left for him.

Jolly, round, red Mr. Sun was just getting ready to go to bed behind the Purple Hills when Mrs. Quack returned. The first Peter knew of her coming was the whistle of her wings as she passed over him. Several times she circled around, high over the Smiling Pool, and Peter simply stared in openmouthed admiration at the speed with which she flew. It didn't seem possible that one so big could move through the air so fast. Twice she set her wings and seemed to just slide down almost to the surface of the Smiling Pool, only to start her stout wings in motion once more and circle around again. It was very clear that she was terribly nervous and suspicious. The third time she landed in the water with a splash and sat perfectly still with her head stretched up, looking and listening with all her might.

"It's all right. There's nothing to be afraid of," said Jerry Muskrat.

"Are you sure?" asked Mrs. Quack anxiously. "I've been fooled too often by men with their terrible guns to ever feel absolutely sure that one isn't hiding and waiting to shoot me." As she spoke she swam about nervously.

"Peter Rabbit and I have been here ever since you left, and I guess we ought to know," replied Jerry Muskrat rather shortly. "There hasn't been anybody near here excepting Farmer Brown's boy, and we told you he wouldn't hurt you."

"He brought us each a carrot," Peter Rabbit broke in eagerly.

"Just the same, I wouldn't trust him," replied Mrs. Quack. "Where is he now?"

"He left ever so long ago, and he won't be back to-night," declared Peter confidently.

"I hope not," said Mrs. Quack, with a sigh. "Did you hear the bang of that terrible gun just after I left here?"

"Yes," replied Jerry Muskrat. "Was it fired at you?"

Mrs. Quack nodded and held up one wing. Peter and Jerry could see that one of the long feathers was missing. "I thought I was flying high enough to be safe," said she, "but when I reached the Big River there was a bang from the bushes on the bank, and something cut that feather out of my wing, and I felt a sharp pain in my side. It made me feel quite ill for a while, and the place is very sore now, but I guess I'm lucky that it was no worse. It is very hard work to know just how far those terrible guns can throw things at you. Next time I will fly higher."

"Where have you been since you left us?" asked Peter.

"Right in the middle of the Big River," replied Mrs. Quack. "It was the only safe place. I didn't dare go near either shore, and I'm nearly starved. I haven't had a mouthful to eat to-day."

Peter opened his mouth to tell her of the wheat and corn left by Farmer Brown's boy and then closed it again. He would let her find it for herself. If he told her about it, she might suspect a trick and refuse to go near the place. He never had seen any one so suspicious, not even Old Man Coyote. But he couldn't blame her, after all she had been through. So he kept still and waited. He was learning, was Peter Rabbit. He was learning a great deal about Mrs. Quack.

VIII

Mrs. Quack Has a Good Meal
and a Rest

There's nothing like a stomach full
　To make the heart feel light;
To chase away the clouds of care
　And make the world seem bright.

THAT'S A FACT. A full stomach makes the whole world seem different, brighter, better, and more worth living in. It is the hardest kind of hard work to be cheerful and see only the bright side of things when your stomach is empty. But once fill that empty stomach, and everything is changed. It was just that way with Mrs. Quack. For days at a time she hadn't had a full stomach because of the hunters with their terrible guns, and when just before dark that night she returned to the Smiling Pool, her stomach was quite empty.

"I don't suppose I'll find much to eat here, but a little in peace and safety is better than a feast with worry and danger," said she, swimming over to the brown, broken-down bulrushes on one side of the Smiling Pool and appearing to stand on her head as she plunged it under water and searched in the mud on the bottom for food. Peter Rabbit looked over at Jerry Muskrat sitting on the Big Rock, and Jerry winked. In a minute up bobbed the head of Mrs. Quack, and there was both a pleased and a worried look on her face. She had found some of the corn left there by Farmer Brown's boy. At once she swam out to the middle of the Smiling Pool, looking suspiciously this way and that way.

"There is corn over there," said she. "Do you know how it came there?"

"I saw Farmer Brown's boy throwing something over there," replied Peter. "Didn't we tell you that he would be good to you?"

"Quack, quack, quack! I've seen that kind of kindness too often to be fooled by it," snapped Mrs. Quack. "He probably saw me leave in a hurry and put this corn here, hoping that I would come back and find it and make up my mind to stay here a while. He thinks that if I do, he'll have a chance to hide near enough to shoot me. I didn't believe this could be a safe place for me, and now I know it. I'll stay here to-night, but to-morrow I'll try to find some other place. Oh, dear, it's dreadful not to have any place at all to feel safe in." There were tears in her eyes.

Peter thought of the dear Old Briar-patch and how safe he always felt there, and he felt a great pity for poor Mrs. Quack, who couldn't feel safe anywhere. And then right away he grew indignant that she should be so distrustful of Farmer Brown's boy, though if he had stopped to think, he would have remembered that once he was just as distrustful.

"I should think," said Peter with a great deal of dignity, "that you might at least believe what Jerry Muskrat and I, who live here all the time, tell you. We ought to know Farmer Brown's boy if any one does, and we tell you that he won't harm a feather of you."

"He won't get the chance!" snapped Mrs. Quack.

Jerry Muskrat sniffed in disgust. "I don't doubt you have suffered a lot from men with terrible guns," said he, "but you don't suppose Peter and I have lived as long as we have without learning a little, do you? I wouldn't trust many of those two-legged creatures myself, but Farmer Brown's boy is different. If all of them were like him, we wouldn't have a thing to fear from them. He has a heart. Yes, indeed, he has a heart. Now you take my advice and eat whatever he has put there for you, be thankful, and stop worrying. Peter and I will keep watch and warn you if there is any danger."

I don't know as even this would have over-come Mrs. Quack's fears if it hadn't been for the taste of that good corn in her mouth, and her empty stomach. She couldn't, she just couldn't resist these, and presently she was back among the rushes, hunting out the corn and wheat as fast as ever she could. When at last she could eat no more, she felt so com-fortable that somehow the Smiling Pool didn't seem such a dangerous place after all, and she quite forgot Farmer Brown's boy. She found a snug hiding-place among the rushes too far out from the bank for Reddy Fox to surprise her, and then with a sleepy "Good night" to Jerry and Peter, she tucked her head under her wing and soon was fast asleep.

Peter Rabbit tiptoed away, and then he hur-ried lipperty-lipperty-lip to the dear Old Briar-patch to tell Mrs. Peter all about Mrs. Quack.

IX

Peter Rabbit Makes an Early Call

PETER RABBIT WAS so full of interest in Mrs. Quack and her troubles that he was back at the Smiling Pool before Mr. Sun had kicked off his rosy blankets and begun his daily climb up in the blue, blue sky. You see, he felt that he had heard only a part of Mrs. Quack's story, and he was dreadfully afraid that she would get away before he could hear the rest. With the first bit of daylight, Mrs. Quack swam out from her hiding-place among the brown rushes. It looked to Peter as if she sat up on the end of her tail as she stretched her neck and wings just as far as she could, and he wanted to laugh right out. Then she quickly ducked her head under water two or three times so that the water rolled down over her back, and again Peter wanted to laugh. But he didn't. He kept perfectly still. Mrs. Quack shook herself and then began to carefully dress her feathers. That is, she care-

fully put back in place every feather that had
been rumpled up. She took a great deal of
time for this, for Mrs. Quack is very neat and
tidy and takes the greatest pride in looking as
fine as she can.

Of course it was very impolite of Peter to
watch her make her toilet, but he didn't think
of that. He didn't mean to be impolite. And
then it was *so* interesting. "Huh!" said he to
himself, "I don't see what any one wants to
waste so much time on their clothes for."

You know Peter doesn't waste any time on
his clothes. In fact, he doesn't seem to care a
bit how he looks. He hasn't learned yet that it
always pays to be as neat and clean as possible and that you must think well of yourself if
you want others to think well of you.

When at last Mrs. Quack had taken a final
shower bath and appeared satisfied that she
was looking her best, Peter opened his mouth
to ask her the questions he was so full of, but
closed it again as he remembered people are
usually better natured when their stomachs
are full, and Mrs. Quack had not yet break-
fasted. So he waited as patiently as he could,
which wasn't patiently at all. At last Mrs.
Quack finished her breakfast, and then she
had to make her toilet all over again. Finally

Peter hopped to the edge of the bank where she would see him.

"Good morning, Mrs. Quack," said he very politely. "I hope you had a good rest and are feeling very well this morning."

"Thank you," replied Mrs. Quack. "I'm feeling as well as could be expected. In fact, I'm feeling better than I have felt for some time in spite of the sore place made by that terrible gun yesterday. You see, I have had a good rest and two square meals, and these are things I haven't had since goodness knows when. This is a very nice place. Let me see, what is it you call it?"

"The Smiling Pool," said Peter.

"That's a good name for it," returned Mrs. Quack. "If only I could be sure that none of those hunters would find me here, and if only Mr. Quack were here, I would be content to stay a while." At the mention of Mr. Quack, the eyes of Mrs. Quack suddenly filled with tears. Peter felt tears of sympathy in his own eyes.

"Where is Mr. Quack?" he asked.

"I don't know," sobbed Mrs. Quack. "I wish I did. I haven't seen him since one of those terrible guns was fired at us over on the Big River yesterday morning a little while before

Little Joe Otter told me about the Smiling Pool. Ever since we started for our home in the far North, I have been fearing that something of this kind might happen. I ought to be on my way there now, but what is the use without Mr. Quack? Without him, I would be all alone up there and wouldn't have any home."

"Won't you tell me all that has happened since you started on your long journey?" asked Peter. "Perhaps some of us can help you."

"I'm afraid you can't," replied Mrs. Quack sadly, "but I'll tell you all about it so that you may know just how thankful you ought to feel that you do not have to suffer what some of us do."

X

How Mr. and Mrs. Quack Started North

PETER RABBIT WAS eager to help Mrs.
Quack in her trouble, though he hadn't
the least idea how he could help and neither
had she. How any one who dislikes water as
Peter does could help one who lives on the
water all the time was more than either one of
them could see. And yet without knowing it,
Peter *was* helping Mrs. Quack. He was giving
her his sympathy, and sympathy often helps
others a great deal more than we even guess.
It sometimes is a very good plan to tell your
troubles to some one who will listen with
sympathy. It was so with Mrs. Quack. She had
kept her troubles locked in her own heart so
long that it did her good to pour them all out
to Peter.

"Mr. Quack and I spent a very comfortable
winter way down in the sunny Southland,"
said she with a far-away look. "It was very
warm and nice down there, and there were a

great many other Ducks spending the winter
with us. The place where we were was far
from the homes of men, and it was only once
in a long while that we had to watch out for
terrible guns. Of course, we had to have our
wits with us all the time, because there are
Hawks and Owls and Minks down there just
as there are up here, but any Duck who can't
keep out of their way deserves to furnish one
of them a dinner.

"Then there was another fellow we had to
watch out for, a queer fellow whom we never
see anywhere but down there. It was never
safe to swim too near an old log floating in the
water or lying on the bank, because it might
suddenly open a great mouth and swallow
one of us whole."

"What's that?" Peter Rabbit leaned forward
and stared at Mrs. Quack with his eyes pop-
ping right out. "What's that?" he repeated.
"How can an old log have a mouth?"

Mrs. Quack just had to smile, Peter was so
in earnest and looked so astonished.

"Of course," said she, "no really truly log
has a mouth or is alive, but this queer fellow I
was speaking of looks so much like an old log
floating in the water unless you look at him
very sharply, that many a heedless young
Duck has discovered the difference when it

was too late. Then, too, he will swim under water and come up underneath and seize you without any warning. He has the biggest mouth I've ever seen, with terrible-looking teeth, and could swallow me whole."

By this time Peter's eyes looked as if they would fall out of his head. "What is his name?" whispered Peter.

"It's Old Ally the 'Gator," replied Mrs. Quack. "Some folks call him Alligator and some just 'Gator, but we call him Old Ally. He's a very interesting old fellow. Some time perhaps I'll tell you more about him. Mr. Quack and I kept out of his reach, you may be sure. We lived quietly and tried to get in as good condition as possible for the long journey back to our home in the North. When it was time to start, a lot of us got together, just as we did when we came down from the North, only this time the young Ducks felt themselves quite grown up. In fact, before we started there was a great deal of love-making, and each one chose a mate. That was a very happy time, a very happy time indeed, but it was a sad time too for us older Ducks, because we knew what dreadful things were likely to happen on the long journey. It is hard enough to lose father or mother or brother or sister, but it is worse to lose a dear mate."

"Some folks call him Alligator and some just 'Gator." *Page 39*.

Mrs. Quack's eyes suddenly filled with tears again. "Oh, dear," she sobbed, "I wish I knew what became of Mr. Quack."

Peter said nothing, but looked the sympathy he felt. Presently Mrs. Quack went on with her story. "We had a splendid big flock when we started, made up wholly of pairs, each pair dreaming of the home they would build when they reached the far North. Mr. Quack was the leader as usual, and I flew right behind him. We hadn't gone far before we began to hear the terrible guns, and the farther we went, the worse they got. Mr. Quack led us to the safest feeding and resting grounds he knew of, and for a time our flock escaped the terrible guns. But the farther we went, the more guns there were." Mrs. Quack paused and Peter waited.

XI

The Terrible, Terrible Guns

"Bang! Bang! Bang! Not a feather spare!
Kill! Kill! Kill! Wound and rip and tear!"

THAT IS WHAT the terrible guns roar from
morning to night at Mrs. Quack and her
friends as they fly on their long journey to
their home in the far North. I don't wonder
that she was terribly uneasy and nervous as
she sat in the Smiling Pool talking to Peter
Rabbit; do you?

"Yes," said she, continuing her story of her
long journey from the sunny Southland where
she had spent the winter, "the farther we got,
the more there were of those terrible guns. It
grew so bad that as well as Mr. Quack knew
the places where we could find food, and no
Duck that ever flew knew them better, he
couldn't find one where we could feel perfectly sure that we were safe. The very safest-
looking places sometimes were the most dan-

gerous. If you saw a lot of Rabbits playing together on the Green Meadows, you would feel perfectly safe in joining them, wouldn't you?"

Peter nodded. "I certainly would," said he. "If it was safe for them it certainly would be safe for me."

"Well, that is just the way we felt when we saw a lot of Ducks swimming about on the edge of one of those feeding-places. We were tired, for we had flown a long distance, and we were hungry. It was still and peaceful there and not a thing to be seen that looked the least bit like danger. So we went straight in to join those Ducks, and then, just as we set our wings to drop down on the water among them, there was a terrible bang, bang, bang, bang! My heart almost stopped beating. Then how we did fly! When we were far out over the water where we could see that nothing was near us we stopped to rest, and there we found only half as many in our flock as there had been."

"Where were the others?" asked Peter, although he guessed.

"Killed or hurt by those terrible guns," replied Mrs. Quack sadly. "And that wasn't the worst of it. I told you that when we started each of us had a mate. Now we found that of those who had escaped, four had lost their mates. They were heartbroken. When it came time for us to move on, they wouldn't go. They said that if they did reach the nesting-place in the far North, they couldn't have nests or eggs or young because they had no mates, so what was the use? Besides, they hoped that if they waited around they might find their mates. They thought they might not have been killed, but just hurt, and might be able to get away from those hunters. So they left us and swam back towards that terrible place, calling for their lost mates, and it was the saddest sound. I know now just how they felt, for I have lost Mr. Quack, and that's why I'm here." Mrs. Quack drew a wing across her eyes to wipe away the tears.

"But what happened to those Ducks that were swimming about there and made you think it was safe?" asked Peter, with a puzzled look on his face.

"Nothing," replied Mrs. Quack. "They had been fastened out there in the water by the hunters so as to make us think it safe, and the terrible guns were fired at us and not at them. The hunters were hidden under grass, and that is why we didn't see them."

Peter blinked his eyes rapidly as if he were having hard work to believe what he had been told. "Why," said he at last, "I never heard of anything so dreadfully unfair in all my life! Do you mean to tell me that those hunters actually made other Ducks lead you into danger?"

"That's just what I mean," returned Mrs. Quack. "Those two-legged creatures don't know what fairness is. Why, some of them have learned our language and actually call us in where they can shoot us. Just think of that! They tell us in our own language that there is plenty to eat and all is safe, so that we will think that other Ducks are hidden and feeding there, and then when we go to join them, we are shot at! You ought to be mighty thankful, Peter Rabbit, that you are not a Duck."

"I am," replied Peter. He knew that not one of the meadow and forest people who were always trying to catch him would do a thing like that.

"It's all true," said Mrs. Quack, "and those hunters do other things just as unfair. Sometimes awful storms will come up, and we just have to find places where we can rest. Those hunters will hide near those places and shoot at us when we are so tired that we can hardly move a wing. It wouldn't be so bad if a hunter would be satisfied to kill just one Duck, just as Reddy Fox is, but he seems to want to kill *every* Duck. Foxes and Hawks and Owls catch a good many young Ducks, just as they do young Rabbits, but you know how we feel about that. They only hunt when they are hungry, and they hunt fairly. When they have got enough to make a dinner, they stop. They keep our wits sharp. If we do not keep out of their way, it is our own fault. It is a kind of game—the game of life. I guess it is Old Mother Nature's way of keeping us wide-awake and sharpening our wits, and so making us better fitted to live.

"With these two-legged creatures with terrible guns, it is all different. We don't have any chance at all. If they hunted us as Reddy Fox does, tried to catch us themselves, it would be different. But their terrible guns kill when we are a long way off, and there isn't any way for us to know of the danger. And then, when one of them does kill a Duck, he isn't satisfied, but keeps on killing and killing and killing. I'm sure one would make him a dinner, if that is what he wants.

"And they often simply break the wings or otherwise terribly hurt the ones they shoot at, and then leave them to suffer, unable to take care of themselves. Oh, dear, I'm afraid that is what has happened to Mr. Quack."

Once more poor Mrs. Quack was quite overcome with her troubles and sorrows. Peter

wished with all his heart that he could do
something to comfort her, but of course he
couldn't, so he just sat still and waited until
she could tell him just what did happen to Mr.
Quack.

XII

What Did Happen to Mr. Quack

"WHEN DID YOU last see Mr. Quack?" asked Jerry Muskrat, who had been listening while Mrs. Quack told Peter Rabbit about her terrible journey.

"Early yesterday morning," replied Mrs. Quack, the tears once more filling her eyes. "We had reached the Big River over there, just six of us out of the big flock that had started from the sunny Southland. How we got as far as that I don't know. But we did, and neither Mr. Quack nor I had lost a feather from those terrible guns that had banged at us all the way up and that had killed so many of our friends.

"We were flying up the Big River, and everything seemed perfectly safe. We were in a hurry, and when we came to a bend in the Big River, we flew quite close to shore, so as not to have to go way out and around. That was where Mr. Quack made a mistake. Even the

48

smartest people will make mistakes sometimes, you know."

Peter Rabbit nodded. "I know," said he. "I've
made them myself." And then he wondered
why Jerry Muskrat laughed right out.

"Yes," continued Mrs. Quack, "that is where
Mr. Quack made a mistake, a great mistake. I
suppose that because not a single gun had
been fired at us that morning he thought perhaps there were no hunters on the Big River.
So to save time he led us close to shore. And
then it happened. There was a bang, bang of a
terrible gun, and down fell Mr. Quack just as
we had seen so many fall before. It was awful.
There was Mr. Quack flying in front of me on
swift, strong wings, and there never was a
swifter, stronger flier or a handsomer Duck
than Mr. Quack, and then all in the wink of an
eye he was tumbling helplessly down, down
to the water below, and I was flying on alone,
for the other Ducks turned off, and I don't
know what became of them. I couldn't stop to
see what became of Mr. Quack, because if I
had, that terrible gun would have killed me.
So I kept on a little way and then turned and
went back, only I kept out in the middle of the
Big River. I dropped down on the water and
swam about, calling and calling, but I didn't

get any answer, and so I don't know what has become of Mr. Quack. I am afraid he was killed, and if he was, I wish I had been killed myself."

Here Mrs. Quack choked up so that she couldn't say another word. Peter's own eyes were full of tears as he tried to comfort her. "Perhaps," said he, "Mr. Quack wasn't killed and is hiding somewhere along the Big River. I don't know why I feel so, but I feel sure that he wasn't killed, and that you will find him yet."

"That's why I've waited instead of going on," replied Mrs. Quack between sobs, "though it wouldn't have been of any use to go on without my dear mate. I'm going back to the Big River now to look for him. The trouble is, I don't dare go near the shore, and if he is alive, he probably is hiding somewhere among the rushes along the banks. I think I'll be going along now, but I'll be back to-night if nothing happens to me. You folks who can always stay at home have a great deal to be thankful for."

"It's lucky for me that Mrs. Peter wasn't here to hear her say that," said Peter, as he and Jerry Muskrat watched Mrs. Quack fly swiftly towards the Big River. "Mrs. Peter is forever worrying and scolding because I don't stay in the dear Old Briar-patch. If she had heard Mrs. Quack say that, I never would have heard the last of it. I wish there was something we could do for Mrs. Quack. I'm going back to the dear Old Briar-patch to think it over, and I guess the sooner I start the better, for that looks to me like Reddy Fox over there, and he's headed this way."

So off for home started Peter, lipperty-lipperty-lip, as fast as he could go, and all the way there he was turning over in his mind what Mrs. Quack had told him and trying to think of some way to help her.

XIII

Peter Tells About Mrs. Quack

To get things done, if you'll but try,
You'll always find there is a way.
What you yourself can't do alone
The chances are another may.

WHEN PETER RABBIT was once more
safely back in the dear Old Briar-patch,
he told Mrs. Peter all about poor Mrs. Quack
and her troubles. Then for a long, long time he
sat in a brown study. A brown study, you
know, is sitting perfectly still and thinking
very hard. That was what Peter did. He sat so
still that if you had happened along, you probably would have thought him asleep. But he
wasn't asleep. No, indeed! He was just thinking and thinking. He was trying to think of
some way to help Mrs. Quack. At last he gave
a little sigh of disappointment.

"It can't be done," said he. "There isn't any
way."

"What can't be done?" demanded a voice right over his head.

Peter looked up. There sat Sammy Jay. Peter had been thinking so hard that he hadn't seen Sammy arrive.

"What can't be done?" repeated Sammy. "There isn't anything that can't be done. There are plenty of things that you can't do, but what you can't do some one else can. Just tuck that fact away in that empty head of yours and never say can't." You know Sammy dearly loves to tease Peter.

Peter made a good-natured face at Sammy. "Which means, I suppose, that what I can't do you can. You always did have a pretty good opinion of yourself, Sammy," said he.

"Nothing of the kind," retorted Sammy. "I simply mean that nobody can do everything, and that very often two heads are better than one. It struck me that you had something on your mind, and I thought I might be able to help you get rid of it. But of course, if you don't want my help, supposing I could and would give it to you, that is an end of the matter, and I guess I'll be on my way. The Old Briar-patch is rather a dull place anyway."

Peter started to make a sharp retort, but thought better of it. Instead he replied mildly:

"Just tuck that fact away in that empty head of yours and never say can't." *Page 53.*

"I was just trying to think of some way to help poor Mrs. Quack."

"Help Mrs. Quack!" exclaimed Sammy in surprise. "Where under the sun did you get acquainted with Mrs. Quack? What's the matter with her? She always has looked to me quite able to help herself."

"Well, she isn't. That is, she needs others to help her just now," replied Peter, "and I've been most thinking my head off trying to find a way to help her." Then he told Sammy how he had met Mrs. Quack at the Smiling Pool and how terrible her long journey up from the sunny Southland had been, and how Mr. Quack had been shot by a hunter with a terrible gun, and how poor Mrs. Quack was quite heartbroken, and how she had gone over to the Big River to look for him but didn't dare go near the places where he might be hiding if he were still alive and hurt so that he couldn't fly, and how cruel and terribly unfair were the men with terrible guns, and all the other things he had learned from Mrs. Quack.

Sammy listened with his head cocked on one side, and for once he didn't interrupt Peter or try to tease him or make fun of him. In fact, as Peter looked up at him, he could see that Sammy was very serious and thoughtful, and that the more he heard of Mrs.

Quack's story the more thoughtful he looked. When Peter finished, Sammy flew down a little nearer to Peter.

"I beg your pardon for saying your head is empty, Peter," said he. "Your heart is right, anyway. Of course, there isn't anything you can do to help Mrs. Quack, but as I told you in the beginning, what you can't do others can. Now I don't say that I can help Mrs. Quack, but I can try. I believe I'll do a little thinking myself."

So Sammy Jay in his turn went into a brown study, and Peter watched him anxiously and a little hopefully.

XIV

Sammy Jay's Plan to Help Mrs. Quack

SAMMY JAY SAT on the lowest branch of a little tree in the dear Old Briar-patch just over Peter Rabbit's head, thinking as hard as ever he could. Peter watched him and wondered if Sammy would be able to think of any plan for helping poor Mrs. Quack. He hoped so. He himself had thought and thought until he felt as if his brains were all mixed up and he couldn't think any more. So he watched Sammy and waited and hoped.

Presently Sammy flirted his wings in a way which Peter knew meant that he had made up his mind. "Did I understand you to say that Mrs. Quack said that if Mr. Quack is alive, he probably is hiding among the rushes along the banks of the Big River?" he asked.

Peter nodded.

"And that she said that she doesn't dare go near the banks because of fear of the terrible guns?"

Again Peter nodded.

"Well, if that's the case, what is the matter with some of us who are not afraid of the terrible guns looking for Mr. Quack?" said Sammy. "I will, for one, and I'm quite sure that my cousin, Blacky the Crow, will, for another. He surely will if he thinks it will spoil the plans of any hunters. Blacky would go a long distance to do that. He hates terrible guns and the men who use them. And he knows all about them. He has very sharp eyes, has Blacky, and he knows when a man has got a gun and when he hasn't. More than that, he can tell better than any one I know of just how near he can safely go to one of those terrible guns. He is smart, my cousin Blacky is, and if he will help me look for Mr. Quack, we'll find him if he is alive."

"That will be splendid!" cried Peter, clapping his hands. "But aren't you afraid of those terrible guns, Sammy?"

"Not when the hunters are trying for Ducks," replied Sammy. "If there is a Duck anywhere in sight, they won't shoot at poor little me or even at Blacky, though they would shoot at him any other time. You see, they know that shooting at us would frighten the Ducks. Blacky knows all about the Big River. In the winter he often gets considerable of his food along its banks. I've been over there a number of times, but I don't know so much about it as he does. Now here is my plan. I'll go find Blacky and tell him all about what we want to do for Mrs. Quack. Then, when Mrs. Quack comes back to the Smiling Pool, if she hasn't found Mr. Quack, we'll tell her what we are going to do and what she must do. She must swim right up the Big River, keeping out in the middle where she will be safe. If there are any hunters hiding along the bank, they will see her, and then they won't shoot at Blacky or me because they will keep hoping that Mrs. Quack will swim in near enough for them to shoot her. Blacky will fly along over one bank of the Big River, and I will do the same over the other bank, keeping as nearly opposite Mrs. Quack as we can. Being up in the air that way and looking down, we will be able to see the hunters and also Mr. Quack, if he is hiding among the rushes. Are you quite sure that Mrs. Quack will come back to the Smiling Pool to-night?"

"She said she would," replied Peter. "Last night she came just a little while before dark, and I think she will do the same thing to-night, to see if any more corn has been left for her. You know Farmer Brown's boy put some there yesterday, and it tasted so good to her that I don't believe she will be able to stay away, even if she wants to. I think your plan is perfectly splendid, Sammy Jay. I do hope Blacky the Crow will help."

"He will. Don't worry about that," replied Sammy. "Hello! There goes Farmer Brown's boy over to the Smiling Pool now."

"Then there will be some more corn for Mrs. Quack. I just know it!" cried Peter. "He is going to see if Mrs. Quack is there, and I just know he has his pockets full of corn."

"I wouldn't mind a little of it myself," said Sammy. "Well, I must go along to hunt up Blacky. Good-by, Peter."

"Good-by and good luck," replied Peter. "I've always said you are not half such a bad fellow as you try to make folks think you are, Sammy Jay."

"Thanks," said Sammy, and started for the Green Forest to look for his cousin, Blacky the Crow.

XV

The Hunt for Mr. Quack

IN SPITE OF her hopelessness in regard to Mr. Quack, there is no doubt that Mrs. Quack felt better that night after she had eaten the corn left among the rushes of the Smiling Pool by Farmer Brown's boy. Now she had that very comfortable feeling that goes with a full stomach, she could think better. As the Black Shadows crept across the Smiling Pool, she turned over in her mind Sammy Jay's plan for helping her the next day. The more she thought about it, the better it seemed, and she began to feel a little ashamed that she had not appeared more grateful to Sammy when he told her. At the time she had been tired and hungry and discouraged. Now she was beginning to feel rested, and she was no longer hungry. These things made all the difference in the world. As she thought over Sammy's plan, she began to feel a little hope, and when at last she put her head under her wing to go to sleep, she had made up her mind that the plan was worth trying, and that she would do her part.

Bright and early the next morning, Sammy Jay and Blacky the Crow were in the Big Hickory-tree near the Smiling Pool ready to start for the Big River to hunt for Mr. Quack. Peter Rabbit had been so afraid that he would miss something that he had stayed near the Smiling Pool all night, so he was on hand to see the start.

It had been agreed that Mrs. Quack was to go to a certain place on the Big River and then swim up as far as she thought it would be of any use. She was to stay in the middle of the river, where she would be quite safe from hunters with terrible guns, and where also these same hunters would be sure to see her and so not be tempted to shoot at Blacky the Crow if he happened to fly over them. You see, they would hope that Mrs. Quack would swim in near enough to be shot and so would not risk frightening her by shooting at Blacky.

When Mrs. Quack had finished her breakfast, she started for the Big River, and her stout wings moved so swiftly that they made a whistling sound. Sammy Jay and Blacky the Crow followed her, but though they flew as fast as they could, Mrs. Quack had reached

the Big River before they had gone half the
way. When they did get there, they saw Mrs.
Quack out in the middle, swimming about and
watching for them. Blacky flew across the
river and pretended to be hunting for food
along the farther bank, just as every hunter
knows he often does. Sammy Jay did the same
thing on the other bank.

Mrs. Quack swam slowly up the Big River,
keeping in the middle, and Blacky and Sammy
followed along up the two banks, all the time
using their sharp eyes for all they were worth
to find Mr. Quack hiding among the broken-
down rushes or under the bushes in the water,
for the Big River had overflowed its banks,
and in some places bushes and trees were in
the water.

Now Sammy Jay dearly loves to hunt for
things. Whenever he knows that one of his
neighbors in the Green Forest has hidden
something, he likes to hunt for it. It isn't so
much that he wants what has been hidden, as
it is that he wants to feel he is smart enough
to find it. When he does find it, he usually
steals it, I'm sorry to say. But it is the fun of
hunting that Sammy enjoys most. So now
Sammy thoroughly enjoyed hunting for Mr.
Quack. He peered into every likely hiding-
place and became so interested that he quite

forgot about the hunters who might be waiting along the bank.

So it happened that he didn't see a boat
drawn in among the bushes until he was right
over it. Sitting in it was a man with a terrible
gun, very intently watching Mrs. Quack out in
the middle of the Big River. Sammy was so
startled that before he thought he opened his
mouth and screamed "Thief! thief! thief!" at
the top of his lungs, and flew away with all his
might. Mrs. Quack heard his scream and
understood just what it meant.

A little later Blacky the Crow discovered
another hunter hiding behind the bushes on
his side. "Caw! caw! caw!" shouted Blacky,
flying out over the water far enough to be safe
from that terrible gun he could see.

"Quack! quack!" replied Mrs. Quack, which
meant that she understood. And so the hunt
went on without a sign of poor Mr. Quack.

XVI

Sammy Jay Sees Something Green

FOR ALL THEIR peeking and peering among the broken-down rushes and under the bushes along the banks of the Big River, and no sharper eyes ever peeked and peered, Sammy Jay and Blacky the Crow had found no sign of the missing Mr. Quack.

"I guess Mrs. Quack was right and that Mr. Quack was killed when he was shot," muttered Sammy to himself. "Probably one of those hunters had him for dinner long ago. Hello! There's another hunter up where the Laughing Brook joins the Big River! I guess I won't take any chances. I'd like to find Mr. Quack, but Sammy Jay is a lot more important to me than Mr. Quack, and that fellow just might happen to take it into his head to shoot at me."

So Sammy silently flew around back of the hunter and stopped in a tree where he could watch all that the man did. For some time

Sammy sat there watching. The hunter was sitting behind a sort of fence of bushes which quite hid him from any one who might happen to be out on the Big River. But of course Sammy could see him perfectly, because he was behind him. Out in front of that little fence, which was on the very edge of the water, were a number of what Sammy at first took to be some of Mrs. Quack's relatives. "Why doesn't he shoot them?" thought Sammy. He puzzled over this as he watched them until suddenly it came into his head that he hadn't seen one of them move since he began watching them. The man changed his position, and still those Ducks didn't move, although some of them were so near that they simply couldn't have helped knowing when the hunter moved unless they were more stupid than any one of Sammy's acquaintance.

This was very curious, very curious indeed. Sammy flew a little nearer and then a little nearer, taking the greatest care not to make a sound. Pretty soon he was so near that he could see those Ducks very plainly, and he stared with all his might. He couldn't see any feathers! No, Sir, he couldn't see any feathers! Then he understood.

"Huh!" said he to himself. "Those are not Ducks at all. They are just pieces of wood made to look like Ducks. Now I wonder what they are for."

In a few minutes he found out. He saw the hunter crouch down a little lower and look down the Big River. Sammy looked too. He saw a flock of real Ducks flying swiftly just above the middle of the Big River. Suddenly the leader turned straight towards the place where the hunter was hiding, and the others followed him. He could hear Mrs. Quack calling excitedly out in the middle of the Big River, but the strangers did not heed her. They had their eyes on those wooden Ducks and were coming straight in to join them.

"They think they are real Ducks and so this place is perfectly safe!" thought Sammy. He saw the hunter make ready to shoot with his terrible gun and then, without stopping to think what might happen to him, he opened his mouth and screamed at the top of his voice. He saw the Ducks suddenly swing out towards the middle of the Big River and knew that they had heard his warning. He saw the hunter suddenly rise and point his gun at the flying Ducks. He heard the bang, bang of the terrible gun, but not one of the flock was hit. The distance was too great. Sammy chuckled happily. Then he remembered that he himself was within easy reach of that terrible gun, and probably the hunter was very angry. In great fright Sammy turned and flew, dodging behind trees and every second expecting to hear again the roar of that terrible gun.

But he didn't, and so when he thought he was safe, he stopped. Now in flying away from the hunter he had followed the Laughing Brook where it winds through a sort of swamp before it joins the Big River. Because there was more water than could be kept between the banks of the Big River, it had crept over the banks, and all the trees of the swamp were standing in water. Just beyond where Sammy was sitting was a pile of brush in the water. A Jolly Little Sunbeam, dancing down through the tree tops, touched something under the edge of the brush, and Sammy's sharp eyes caught a flash of green. Idly he watched it, and presently it moved. Instantly Sammy was all curiosity. He flew over where he could see better.

"Now what can that be?" thought Sammy, as he peered down at the pile of brush and tried to see under it.

XVII

Mr. Quack Is Found at Last

SAMMY JAY'S EYES sparkled as he
watched that spot of green under the pile
of brush in the swamp through which the
Laughing Brook finds its way to join the Big
River. All around was water, for you know it
was spring, and the melting snows on the hills
way up where the Big River has its beginning
were pouring more water into the Big River
than its banks would hold as it hurried down
to the Great Ocean. It just couldn't hurry fast
enough to take all that water down as fast as
it ran into the Big River, and so the water had
crept over the banks in places. It had done
this right here in the little swamp where
Sammy was.

Sammy sat perfectly still, for he learned
long ago that only by keeping perfectly still
may one see all that is to be seen. That green
spot had moved. He was sure of that. And
if it moved, it must be something alive. If it

were alive, it must be somebody, and Sammy
wanted to know who it was. Try as he would
he couldn't remember any one who wore such
glossy green as that. So he sat perfectly still,
for he knew that if whoever was hiding under
that brush should even guess that he was
being watched, he would not come out.

So, his eyes sparkling with excitement,
Sammy watched. He was impatiently patient.
Did you know that it is possible to be impatiently patient? Well, it is. Sammy was just
boiling with impatience inside, but he didn't
let that impatience spoil the patience of his
waiting. He sat there just as still as still, with
his eyes fixed on that green spot, and you
would never have guessed that he was fairly
bursting with impatience to know who it was
he was watching. That is what is called self-
control. It means the power to make yourself
do a certain thing, no matter how much you
may want to do something else. It is a splendid thing to have, is self-control.

After what seemed to Sammy a very long
time, the green spot moved again. Little by little something reached out from under the pile
of brush. It was a head, a very beautiful green
head, and it was exactly like Mrs. Quack's
head, only hers was a sober brown instead of
green. Sammy choked back a little gasp of

surprise as a sudden thought popped into his head. Could this be the lost Mr. Quack? He had forgotten that probably Mr. Quack dressed differently from Mrs. Quack, and so of course he had been looking for some one all in brown.

There was the bang of a gun somewhere over on the Big River, and the green head was hastily withdrawn under the bush, but not before Sammy had seen a look of terrible fear in his eyes. "I believe it *is* Mr. Quack!" thought Sammy. "If it is, I'll have the best news ever to tell Mrs. Quack. Just trust Sammy Jay to find anything he goes looking for."

This was just plain boasting, and Sammy knew it. But Sammy always does have a good opinion of himself. It is one of his faults. He quite lost sight of the fact that it was entirely by accident that he had come over to this swamp. Now that he had guessed who this might be, he was less impatient. He waited as still as you please, and at last the green head was slowly stretched out again, and Sammy could see that the neck was green, too, and that around the neck was a white collar. Sammy could keep still no longer.

"Are you Mr. Quack?" he asked eagerly.

The beautiful head disappeared like a flash. Sammy waited a minute or two, before he

"Yes," said he in a low voice, "I am Mr. Quack."
Page 73.

repeated his question, adding: "You needn't be afraid. There isn't anybody here but me, and I'm your friend. I just want to know if you are Mr. Quack because I've been looking for you for Mrs. Quack. Are you?"

Slowly, looking this way and that way with fear and suspicion in his eyes, a handsome Duck came out from under the pile of brush. "Yes," said he in a low voice, "I am Mr. Quack. Where is Mrs. Quack?"

"Safe and sound over on the Big River," replied Sammy joyfully. "Oh, I'm so glad I've found you!"

XVIII

Sammy Jay Sends Mrs. Quack
to the Swamp

WHEN SAMMY JAY left Mr. Quack in the swamp over by the bank of the Big River, he flew straight back to the Smiling Pool. At first he thought of flying out over the Big River and screaming the news to Mrs. Quack, who, you know, was swimming about out there. But he knew that if he did, she would very likely fly right over where Mr. Quack was, and that wouldn't do at all. No, indeed, that wouldn't do at all. One of the hunters would be sure to see her. So Sammy wisely flew back to the Smiling Pool to wait until Mrs. Quack should come back there for the night.

Of course he told Peter Rabbit all about Mr. Quack, and Peter was so delighted at the thought that Mr. Quack was alive that he capered about in quite the craziest way. "Does Mrs. Quack know yet?" asked Peter.

Sammy shook his head. "I'm going to tell her when she comes back here to-night," he explained. "I was afraid if I told her before then she would fly straight to him and perhaps get them both in trouble."

"Quite right, Sammy! Quite right!" Peter exclaimed. "I wouldn't have thought of that. My, won't she be happy when you do tell her! I wonder what she'll say and what she'll do. I'm going to stay right here so as to see her when she hears the good news. Here comes your cousin, Blacky the Crow. Does he know yet?"

"No," replied Sammy, "but I'm going to tell him as soon as he gets here." They watched Blacky draw nearer and nearer, and as soon as he was within hearing Sammy shouted the news. Caw, caw, caw," replied Blacky, hurrying a little faster.

As soon as he reached the Big Hickory-tree, Sammy told the whole story over again, and Blacky was quite as glad as the others. While they waited for Mrs. Quack he told how he had hunted and hunted along the farther bank of the Big River and how he had seen the hunters with their terrible guns hiding and had warned Mrs. Quack just where each one was.

Jolly, round, red Mr. Sun was getting ready

to go to bed behind the Purple Hills and the Black Shadows were beginning to creep out over the Green Meadows before Mrs. Quack came. In fact, Sammy Jay and Blacky were getting very uneasy. It was almost bed-time for them, for neither of them dared stay out after dark. They had almost made up their minds to leave Peter to tell the news when they saw Mrs. Quack coming swiftly from the direction of the Big River. She looked so sad and discouraged that even Blacky the Crow was sorry for her, and you know Blacky isn't much given to such feelings.

"What's the news, Mrs. Quack?" asked Peter, his eyes dancing.

"There isn't any," replied Mrs. Quack.

"Oh, yes, there is!" cried Sammy Jay, who couldn't possibly keep still any longer.

"What is it?" demanded Mrs. Quack eagerly, and it seemed to Peter that there was a wee bit of hope in her voice.

"Did you happen to notice that just before the Laughing Brook joins the Big River it flows through a little swamp?" asked Sammy.

Mrs. Quack nodded her head rapidly. "What of it?" she demanded.

"Nothing much, only if I were you I would go down there after dark," replied Sammy.

Mrs. Quack looked up at Sammy sharply. "Why should I go down there?" she asked.

"If I tell you, will you wait until I get quite through?" asked Sammy in his turn.

Mrs. Quack promised that she would.

"Well, then," replied Sammy, "this afternoon I found a stranger hiding in there, a stranger with a beautiful green head and neck and a white collar."

"Mr. Quack! Oh, it was Mr. Quack!" cried Mrs. Quack joyfully and lifted her wings as if she would start for the swamp at once.

"Stop!" cried Sammy sharply. "You said you would wait until I am through. It won't do for you to go there until after dark, because there is a hunter hiding very near Mr. Quack's hiding-place. Wait until it is dark and he has gone home. Then take my advice, and when you have found Mr. Quack, bring him right up here to the Smiling Pool. He can't fly, but he can swim up the Laughing Brook, and this is the safest place for both of you. Now good night and good luck."

Jerry Muskrat's Great Idea

A friendly friend is a friend indeed
When he proves a friend in the time of need.

MR. AND MRS. QUACK had been so much taken up with each other and with their troubles that they had quite forgotten they were not alone in the Smiling Pool, which they had reached by swimming up the Laughing Brook. So it happened that when Mrs. Quack suggested that if Mr. Quack's wing got strong they might be able to find a lonesome pond not too far away where they could make their home for the summer, they were a little startled to hear a voice say: "I know where there is one, and you will not have to fly at all to get to it." Both jumped a little. You see their nerves had been very much upset for a long time, and the least unexpected thing made them jump. Then both laughed.

"Hello, Jerry Muskrat! We'd forgotten all about you," said Mrs. Quack. "What was that you said?"

Jerry good-naturedly repeated what he had said. Mrs. Quack's face brightened. "Do you really mean it?" she asked eagerly. "Do you really mean that you know of a pond where we could live and not be likely to be seen by these two-legged creatures called men?"

"That's what I said," replied Jerry briefly.

"Oh, Jerry, you're not joking, are you? Tell me you're not joking," begged Mrs. Quack.

"Of course I'm not joking," returned Jerry just a little bit indignantly. "I am not the kind of a fellow to joke people who are in such trouble as you and Mr. Quack seem to be in. The idea came to me while you were talking. I couldn't help overhearing what you were saying, and the minute you mentioned a lonesome pond, the idea came to me, and I think it's a perfectly splendid idea. I know of just the lonesomest kind of a lonesome pond, and you won't have to fly a stroke to get to it. If you are smart enough not to be caught by Reddy Fox or Hooty the Owl or Billy Mink or any of those people who hunt for a living, there isn't any reason I know of why you shouldn't spend the summer there in peace and comfort."

Mrs. Quack's eyes fairly shone with hope and eagerness. "Oh, Jerry, tell us where it is, and we'll start for it right away!" she cried.

Jerry's eyes twinkled. "Of course, the owner of that pond might not like to have neighbors. I hadn't thought of that," said he. "Perhaps he ought to be asked first."

Mrs. Quack's face fell. "Who is the owner?" she asked.

"My cousin, Paddy the Beaver. He made it," replied Jerry proudly.

Mrs. Quack's face lighted up again at once. "I'm sure he won't object," said she. "We know a great many of the Beaver family. In fact, they are very good neighbors of ours in our home in the far Northland. I didn't suppose there was a Beaver pond anywhere around here. Tell me where it is, Jerry, and I'll go right up there and call on your cousin."

"All you've got to do is to follow the Laughing Brook way back into the Green Forest, and you'll come to Paddy's pond," said he. "He made that pond himself two years ago. He came down from the Great Woods and built a dam across the Laughing Brook way back there in the Green Forest and gave us a great scare here in the Smiling Pool by cutting off the water for a few days. He has got a very nice pond there now. Honker the Goose and his flock spent a night in it on their way south last fall."

Mrs. Quack waited to hear no more. She shot up into the air and disappeared over the tops of the trees in the Green Forest.

"What do you think of my idea?" asked Jerry, as he and Mr. Quack watched her out of sight.

"I think it is great, just simply great," replied Mr. Quack.

XX

Happy Days for Mr. and Mrs. Quack

Whose heart is true and brave and strong,
   Who ne'er gives up to grim despair,
Will find some day that skies are blue
   And all the world is bright and fair.

IF YOU DON'T believe it, just ask Mr. and
Mrs. Quack. They know. Certainly the
world never looked darker for any one than it
did for them when the terrible gun of a hunter
broke Mr. Quack's wing on the Big River and
ended all their dreams of a home in the far
Northland. Then, through the help of Jerry
Muskrat, they found the lonely pond of Paddy
the Beaver deep in the Green Forest, and
there, because their secret had been well
kept, presently they found peace and hope
and then happiness. You see, the heart of Mrs.
Quack was true and brave and strong. She
was the kind to make the best of things, and

she at once decided that if they couldn't have their home where they wanted it, they would have it where they could have it. She was determined that they should have a home anyway, and Paddy the Beaver's little pond was not such a bad place after all.

So she wasted no time. She examined every inch of the shore of that little pond. At last, a little back from the water, she found a place to suit her, a place so well hidden by bushes that only the sharpest eyes ever would find it. And a little later it would be still harder to find, as she well knew, for all about clumps of tall ferns were springing up, and when they had fully unfolded, not even the keen eyes of Sammy Jay looking down from a near-by tree would be able to discover her secret. There she made a nest on the ground, a nest of dried grass and leaves, and lined it with the softest and most beautiful of linings, down plucked from her own breast. In it she laid ten eggs. Then came long weeks of patient sitting on them, watching the wonder of growing things about her, the bursting into bloom of shy wood flowers, the unfolding of leaves on bush and tree, the springing up in a night of queer mushrooms, which people call toadstools, and all the time dreaming beautiful Duck dreams

of the babies which would one day hatch
from those precious eggs. She never left them
save to get a little food and just enough exer-
cise to keep her well and strong, and when
she did leave them, she always carefully
pulled soft down over them to keep them
warm while she was away.

Mr. Quack knew all about that nest, though
he had taken no part in building it and had no
share in the care of those eggs. He was very
willing that she should do all the work and
thought it quite sufficient that he should be on
guard to give warning if danger should
appear. So he spent the long beautiful days
lazily swimming about in the little pond, gossiping with Paddy the Beaver, and taking the
best of care of himself. The broken wing
healed and grew strong again, for it had not
been so badly broken, after all. If he missed
the company of others of his kind which he
would have had during these long days of
waiting had they been able to reach their
usual nesting-place in the far Northland, he
never mentioned it.

Unknown to them, Farmer Brown's boy discovered where they were. Later he came often
to the pond and was content to sit quietly on
the shore and watch Mr. Quack, so that Mr.

Those were happy days indeed for Mr. and Mrs.
Quack in the pond of Paddy the Beaver. *Page 86.*

Quack grew quite used to him and did not fear him at all. In fact, after the first few times, he made no attempt to hide. You see he discovered that Farmer Brown's boy was a friend. Always after he had left, there was something good to eat near where he had been sitting, for Farmer Brown's boy brought corn and oats and sometimes a handful of wheat.

He knew, and Mr. Quack knew that he knew, that somewhere near was a nest, but he did not try to find it much as he longed to, for he knew that would frighten and worry Mrs. Quack. So the dear, precious secret of Mr. and Mrs. Quack was kept, for not even Paddy the Beaver knew just where that nest was, and in due time, early one morning, Mrs. Quack proudly led forth for their first swim ten downy, funny ducklings. Oh, those were happy days indeed for Mr. and Mrs. Quack in the pond of Paddy the Beaver, and in their joy they quite forgot for a time the terrible journey which had brought them there. But finally the Ducklings grew up, and when Jack Frost came in the fall, the whole family started on the long journey to the sunny Southland. I hope they got there safely, don't you?

Among those whom Mr. and Mrs. Quack came to know very well while they lived in the pond of Paddy the Beaver was that funny fellow who wears rings on his tail—Bobby Coon. In the next book I will tell you of some of Bobby's adventures.*

THE END.

---

*NOTE: *The Adventures of Bobby Raccoon* is published by Dover Publications, (0-486-28617-7).

CHILDREN'S THRIFT CLASSICS

Just $1.00

All books complete and unabridged, except where noted.
96pp., 5³/₁₆″ × 8¼″, paperbound.